# Chapter 1
## My Early Childhood

I was born on a Friday night at twelve o'clock. I have been told that I uttered my first cry as the clock began to strike midnight.

That Friday afternoon my mother was sitting by the fire feeling sad and afraid when she noticed a strange lady walking up the path towards the door. The woman, however, did not ring the door bell but came and looked in at the window with the end of her nose pressing so hard against the glass that it soon became flat and white. My mother, who was in poor health, was so

surprised that she fell into a faint. When my mother recovered she saw that the woman had entered the room and was now standing by the window.

Although they had never met, my mother realised that the woman was my father's aunt. Her name was Miss Trotwood, or Miss Betsey, as my poor mother called her. My father had died six months before I was born, but he had been her favourite nephew up to the time of his marriage. However, when he married my mother, a girl not yet twenty, Miss Betsey had left for her cottage by the sea and she and my father never saw each other again.

Miss Betsey turned to my mother and said,

"Now, child, from the moment this girl is born. . . ."

"Perhaps boy," my mother said timidly.

"A girl, it must be a girl," said Miss

Betsey, "and I intend to call her Betsey Trotwood Copperfield."

"Oh, dear," said my mother weakly. "I'm in such a tremble I shall die."

"No, no, no," Miss Betsey said firmly. "Have some tea."

Then she opened the parlour-door and called,

"Peggotty, bring some tea. Your mistress is rather unwell."

Peggotty brought the tea and, as it was now quite dark in the parlour, she lit the candles. She saw at once how ill my mother was and quickly took her upstairs to bed. Then she hurried to get the doctor.

Several hours later Doctor Chillip, who was an extremely mild and timid, little man, came down from my mother's room to announce my birth. Without a word, my aunt, Miss Betsey, seized her bonnet by the

strings and struck the poor doctor on the head. Then she walked out, never to return.

So my life began.

As I look back, I remember my dear mother with her beautiful hair and youthful shape, and I remember dark-eyed Peggotty, who had no shape at all. I remember playing in the winter twilight in our cosy parlour and the pity I used to feel for my father's gravestone lying alone in the dark churchyard nearby. I remember dancing about the parlour and when my mother was out of breath she would sit down to rest and I used to watch her winding her shiny curls round her fingers. They were happy times; my mother called me her "little Davy" and she taught me my lessons and loved me well.

## Chapter 2
### I Experience a Change in My Life

One night, not long after my eighth birthday, Peggotty and I were sitting by the parlour fire waiting for my mother to come home. I had been reading to Peggotty about crocodiles. I must have read badly for, after I had done, she seemed to think that crocodiles, or "crorkindills" as she insisted on calling them, were some kind of vegetable.

Some time later my mother returned with a gentleman who had escorted us home from church the previous Sunday. During the next two months, Mr Murdstone – I knew him by

that name now – was a frequent visitor. Gradually, I became used to seeing him, but I did not like him or his dark eyes and deep voice. I also noticed a strange look on Peggotty's face whenever he appeared.

"Master Davy," she said to me one evening when my mother was out. "How should you like to go along with me and spend a fortnight at my brother's house in Yarmouth?" Then she added coaxingly, "There's the sea and the ships and boats and the fishermen and the beach and my nephew, Ham, to play with."

"That would indeed be a treat," I said, "but what about Mamma? I can't leave her by herself."

When Peggotty answered, I saw that strange look come over her face again.

"Bless you, Master Davy!" she said. "Don't you know that your mother is going off on a visit herself?"

Peggotty and I were to travel to Yarmouth in a carrier's cart. When the day came for us to leave, my mother kissed me and we left her standing in the road, waving good-bye. As I looked back I saw Mr Murdstone come up to my mother and I wondered what business it was of his to be there.

As we drove along, Peggotty and Mr Barkis, the jovial cart-driver, laughed and chatted happily. It was a long journey and when we got into the streets of Yarmouth I smelled the fish, the pitch and the tar and I saw carts jingling up and down over the stones and sailors walking about.

Peggotty's nephew, Ham, was waiting for us at the inn. He was a huge, strong fellow, some six feet tall, but with the face of a young boy. With Ham carrying me on his back and a box of ours under his arm, and Peggotty carrying another small box, we made our way past gas-works, shipyards, rope-walks, smiths' forges, riggers' lofts and a great many other such places, until we came out upon a flat waste that lay by the sea.

Then Ham spoke,

"Yon's our house, Mas'r Davy!" he said.

I looked in all directions and saw no house but, not far off, there was a black barge, high and dry on the ground, with a door cut in the side and some tiny windows too. There was an iron funnel sticking out of it for a chimney and this was smoking very cosily.

"Is that it?" I asked. "That ship-looking thing?"

"That's it, Mas'r Davy," said Ham.

If the barge had been Aladdin's cave I could not have been more bewitched with the idea of living in it. Peggotty showed me my bedroom in the stern of the barge. She opened a little door and I saw a tiny window where the rudder used to go through. There

was a very small bed, which there was just room enough to get into, and on the wall, at just the right height for me, there was a mirror, framed with sea-shells. A posy of seaweed in a blue mug on the table completed the most delightful bedroom I had ever seen.

We were welcomed by Mrs Gummidge, a very kindly lady in a white apron, and by Emily, a beautiful little girl with golden curls and blue eyes. Later, Peggotty informed me that the widowed Mrs Gummidge had been Mr Peggotty's housekeeper since the death of her husband. She also told me that Ham and Emily, a nephew and niece orphaned in their childhoods, had been adopted by her brother, Mr Peggotty.

"Good as gold and true as steel Mr Peggotty is," she said affectionately.

When I met Mr Peggotty I could tell at once that he was a kind and good-natured man.

"Glad to see you, sir," he said. "You'll find us rough, sir, but you'll find us ready. We shall be proud of your company."

Early next morning I was out of bed and out with little Emily, picking up stones on the beach. I told her my father had died before I was born and that my mother and I had always lived by ourselves. Emily told me she had first lost her mother, and then her father, who was drowned at sea.

Emily and I spent many happy hours playing on the beach and talking. We often went with Ham to look at the boats and ships and sometimes he took us for a row. So the days slipped by and I was completely in love with little Emily long before my visit was over. During my stay I had thought little about my home and, when the day came for me to leave, I said a tearful good-bye to Emily and promised to write to her. On the return journey Peggotty seemed deeply

troubled by her thoughts and again I saw that strange look come over her face. The nearer to home we drew, the more excited I became about seeing my mother again but, when we arrived, it was a strange servant who met us at the door and I suddenly felt very frightened. Then Peggotty took me by the hand, led me into the kitchen and closed the door.

"Peggotty! Where's Mamma? Mamma's not dead, is she?" I cried in fright.

"No, Master Davy, she's not dead. Your mamma has re-married and you have a new pa. Now come and see him," said Peggotty.

"No! No! I don't want to see him," I yelled.

"Then come and see your mamma," Peggotty said quietly. We went to the parlour, whereupon she left me. My mother was sitting by the fire and the forbidding Mr Murdstone was at her side. When my mother jumped up to greet me he told her to control

herself, so I went and kissed her and she kissed me but rather timidly, I thought. Then Mr Murdstone shook hands with me, but I crept out of the parlour at the first opportunity for I felt uneasy in his presence.

My unease soon turned to a hatred and fear of Mr Murdstone for his arrival had brought many changes to our lives. My old bedroom was changed and I had to sleep far away from my mother who now hugged and kissed me only when Mr Murdstone was elsewhere. His strictness was hard to bear and Peggotty comforted me when she could.

Then, one day, a gloomy-looking lady came to live with us; she was Miss Jane Murdstone, Mr Murdstone's elder sister. She soon made it clear that she did not like boys and my life became even more miserable. My father had left a small collection of books and I quickly took to spending my days reading alone in my room.

There had been some talk between Mr Murdstone and his sister of sending me away to boarding school but, as yet, they were undecided. Meanwhile, I was to continue learning my lessons from my mother. In the past I had been a good student but the menacing presence of Mr Murdstone and his sister made me so nervous that I could hardly recite my lessons at all. Mr Murdstone decided to discipline me for my failures. He took me to my room and quickly put me across his knee.

"Mr Murdstone! Sir! Don't! Pray, don't beat me," I cried out. "I have tried to learn, sir, but I can't learn while you and Miss Murdstone are near. I can't!"

"Can't, David? Can't? We'll soon see about that," he said sharply. Then he struck me so violently with his cane that I cried out in pain and begged him to stop but he hit me again and again. I suddenly caught

the hand that held me and bit it through. He beat me then as if he meant to beat me to death. I heard my mother and Peggotty crying bitterly. Then he was gone, the door was locked and I was alone. For the next five days I was a prisoner in my own room. Miss Murdstone brought me food but I saw no one else, not even my mother. On the last night, Peggotty came to my door and whispered through the keyhole,

"Master Davy, tomorrow you are to leave for a boarding school near London. I will take care of your mother and I will never forget you."

Then, as she couldn't kiss me, Peggotty kissed the keyhole and slipped quietly away. In the morning when I was brought downstairs, I saw my mother. She was very pale and her eyes were red and swollen. I ran into her arms but she held me hurriedly for Mr Murdstone was near. Then Mr Barkis, the carrier, arrived. My box was lifted into the cart and we set off. We had gone perhaps half a mile along the road when, to my astonishment, Peggotty burst from the bushes and climbed into the cart. She took me in her arms and held me close but said nothing. Presently, she gave me three shillings and some bags of cakes. She also handed me two half-crowns wrapped in a note from my mother. Then, after a final hug, she was down from the cart and gone.

On the journey to Yarmouth Mr Barkis questioned me about Peggotty. When he learned that she was not married, he asked me to give her a message when I was next writing to her. The message puzzled me.

"Say that Barkis is willin', would you? Barkis is willin'," he said.

Much later I was to learn that Barkis wanted to marry Peggotty.

When we reached Yarmouth Mr Barkis

left me at the coach yard where I boarded the night coach to London. We arrived at about eight the next morning but there was nobody there to meet a child by the name of Murdstone, or Copperfield. I had just decided to start walking back home when a pale, young man came up to me.

"You must be the new boy?" he said. "I'm Mr Mell, one of the masters at Salem House."

When we arrived I saw that the school was empty for I had been sent there in holiday-time as a punishment for my wrong-doing. And, as a further punishment, I had always to carry a sign on my back which read: 'Take care of him. He bites.'.

# Chapter 3
## My 'First Half' at Salem House School

For the first month I had lessons every day with Mr Mell. I did them without disgrace for there were no Mr and Miss Murdstone to fear. Then, one evening, I was brought before the headmaster, Mr Creakle. His face was fiery and he was bald on the top of his head. He had a large chin, a little nose and sunken eyes. He spoke in a whisper.

"So!" he said. "This is the young gentleman whose teeth should be filed to stop him from biting!"

Then, taking me by the ear, he whispered,

"I have the happiness of knowing Mr Murdstone, your worthy stepfather, and he knows I always do my duty."

So saying, he gave my ear a savage twist and ordered me out of his study.

It was fortunate for me that Tommy Traddles was the first boy who returned to school. He so enjoyed my sign that he made a joke of it for the other boys which saved me from further embarrassment.

I was soon introduced to a very good-looking boy called James Steerforth, an excellent student and my senior by at least six years. He told me that I, as a new boy, was expected to provide a secret feast for the others. He offered to buy some biscuits, some fruit and a bottle of currant wine.

"I can go out whenever I please and I'll smuggle it in," said Steerforth.

I was worried about spending all my money but, nevertheless, I gave it to him. Later

that night a splendid feast was laid out on my bed. I sat near Steerforth and the other boys grouped around us on the nearest beds and on the floor. How well I recall our sitting there, talking in whispers about the school and the masters. We talked late into the night. Then Steerforth told me that he would always take care of me and I was grateful for his friendship.

The next day school began in earnest. There was a sudden and deathly silence when Mr Creakle entered the schoolroom. He came to where I sat.

"This is the young man who is famous for biting," he said. "Well, now you will see that I am famous for biting, too."

And, as if to prove it, he beat me and most of the other boys too during that first day and in the days that followed. My one comfort was the early removal of my sign which was in the way of his cane.

Poor Traddles was always being caned; I think he was caned every day that half-year. But, strangely, Mr Creakle never ventured to lay a hand on James Steerforth.

I felt proud to know Steerforth and he continued his protection of me. One afternoon I told him of the wonderful stories I had read in my father's books and, when he·realised that I remembered them still, he said,

"I tell you what, young Copperfield, you shall tell 'em to me for I can't get to sleep very early at night. We'll go over 'em one after another. We'll make a regular Arabian Nights of it."

I began telling my stories that very night and, before long, Traddles was adding sound effects to the comic parts. In return, Steerforth helped me with my sums and anything in my lessons that was too hard for me.

Despite the harsh regime at Salem House I made progress for I was a good reader and I was anxious to learn. So the days passed and when the holidays came I found that I was to go home.

## Chapter 4
## My Tenth Birthday

I was met at the coach station by Mr Barkis. He welcomed me as if not five minutes had passed since we were last together. As soon as I was seated in the cart, he asked about Peggotty.

"I gave Peggotty your message when I wrote to her," I told him. But he didn't mention her again.

When we arrived at the house, he left me at the gate. I walked slowly up the path, fearing at every step to see the scowling faces of Mr or Miss Murdstone at a window.

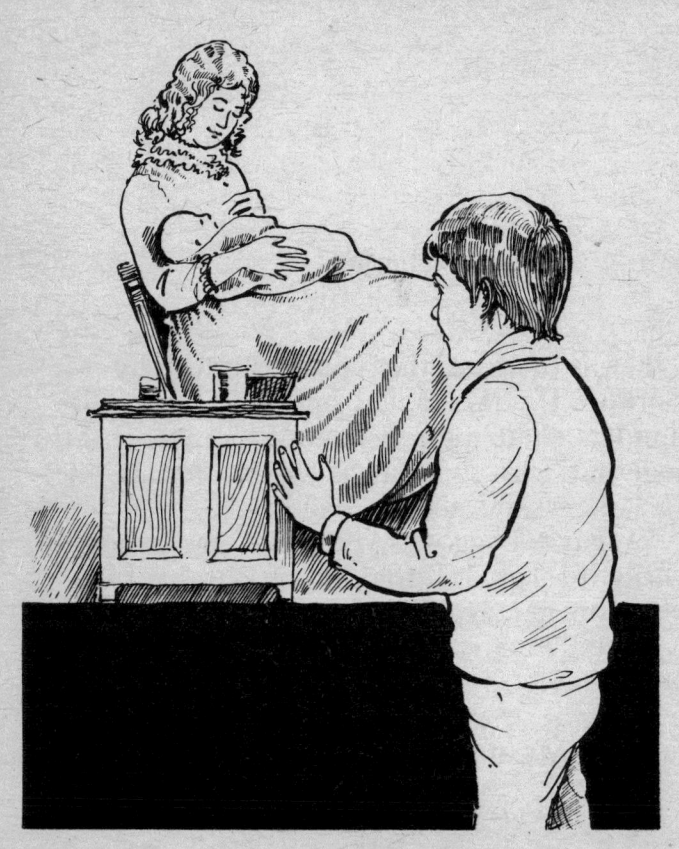

When I reached the door I heard my mother's voice. She was singing quietly. I went softly into the parlour and found her sitting by the fire. She was feeding a tiny infant.

"Come, Davy," she said. "He is your new baby brother."

As Mr and Miss Murdstone were out, and not expected to return before night, my mother, Peggotty and I dined together by the fireside. When I told Peggotty about Mr Barkis, she laughed and threw her apron over her face.

"Oh, drat the man!" she cried. "He wants to marry me. I wouldn't have him. Indeed, I wouldn't have anybody."

"Peggotty, dear," said my mother, affectionately, "you should marry some day, but don't leave me yet."

"I'll stay with you always," cried Peggotty. "And when I'm too deaf, too lame and too blind to be of any use I shall go to my Davy and ask him to take me in."

"And I'll make you as welcome as a queen," I said.

We sat round the fire and talked. When my baby brother was awake, I nursed him in my arms; when he was asleep, my mother held me tenderly and I was happy once more, though not for long. Miss Murdstone soon put a stop to my holding my brother and to my spending time in the kitchen with Peggotty, so I sat wearily in the parlour day after day. The holidays finally came to an end and, although I felt sad when I left my mother at the garden gate, I was not sorry to go.

Two months passed. Then, on the morning of my tenth birthday, I was summoned into the parlour at Salem House. As I expected a hamper from Peggotty, I hurried, but there I found Mrs Creakle with an opened letter in her hand. She led me to the sofa and sat down beside me.

"David Copperfield," she said gravely, "I'm sorry to tell you that your mother and brother are dead."

Mrs Creakle was kind to me. She kept me in the parlour all day. I cried until I wore myself to sleep and when I awoke I cried again. The next day I went home. I was in Peggotty's arms before I got to the door and I was comforted to learn that it was my own, dear Peggotty who had nursed my mother during her last days.

I was measured and fitted for my mourning suit. My mother and my little brother were buried less than a week later and I was left feeling more lost and lonely than ever before.

The day after the funeral Miss Murdstone gave Peggotty a month's notice. As to me, or my future, not a word was said. In fact

Mr and Miss Murdstone preferred to ignore me as much as they could.

Peggotty was unable to find a suitable position nearby so she decided to go to Yarmouth to live with her brother.

"Davy," she said. "Perhaps you will be allowed to go along with me for a visit."

When I sought permission to go, Miss Murdstone readily gave her consent for no doubt she was pleased to get me out of the house. So, when the month was up, I left with Peggotty. Mr Barkis smiled at Peggotty and we travelled happily to Yarmouth. I told Mr Peggotty, Ham and little Emily about school and about my new friends, Steerforth and Traddles. The days passed much as they had passed before. Everyone was very kind to me and no one mentioned my poor mother's death.

Towards the end of my holiday Emily and I went for a ride in the cart with Peggotty

and Mr Barkis. Before long, we stopped at a church and Barkis went in with Peggotty, leaving little Emily and me alone in the cart. A good while later they came out and told us that they were now married. They were to live in Barkis's cottage. Peggotty told me that she had made ready a special room for me.

"Master Davy," she said. "You will always be welcome in my house and your 'crorkindill' book will be on the shelf waiting to be read."

I thanked Peggotty, my dear old nurse, with all my heart.

The next day I went home. Mr and Miss Murdstone disliked me and they coldly and sullenly neglected me. I missed my mother and I missed Peggotty. I was so miserable that I longed to be sent back to school. But Mr Murdstone said he could not afford it and I was to be sent to London to work.

Mr Murdstone and a friend of his owned

a warehouse and I was to go there. I would earn seven shillings a week – just enough to feed and clothe myself. I would lodge with a family who lived near the warehouse and Mr Murdstone was to pay for my room.

Thus it was that I found myself, at ten years old, on the way to London to begin life on my own.

## Chapter 5
## I Begin Life on My Own

Murdstone and Grinby's warehouse was at the waterside, down a narrow street in Blackfriars. It was a dilapidated old house; its rooms made filthy by the dirt and smoke of a hundred years and now overrun with rats. I met three or four other boys on my first morning. We were employed to rinse and wash wine bottles and, when the empty bottles ran short, we pasted labels on full ones, or fitted corks, or packed the finished bottles in casks. So the morning went by and at half-past twelve precisely Mr Grinby tapped at the window and I was beckoned to go into his office. I went in. A stoutish, middle-aged person, with no more hair on his head than there is on an egg, stood there.

"This is Mr Micawber," said Mr Grinby to me.

"Ahem!" said the stranger. "That is my name. And you, young sir, are Master David Copperfield, the boy whom I have now the pleasure to receive as a lodger in my house. And I shall be happy to call this evening to show you the nearest way to my house."

He spoke with a flourish that belied his shabby appearance.

Mr Micawber came for me at eight o'clock. I washed my hands and face and we walked together to a shabby, old house in City Road. There, he presented me to Mrs Micawber, a thin and faded lady, who was sitting in the parlour with their four small children.

She told me that Mr Micawber had debts he could not pay.

"Mr Micawber's difficulties are almost overwhelming and I don't know whether it is possible to bring him through them," she said.

The Micawbers were kind to me but I still felt sad and lonely. I worked at the warehouse all day and had to support myself on the money I earned. I had no friends and no one to turn to for advice or encouragement. I was without hope and I feared that I would forget everything I had learned at school. Life on my own was hard and I cried often but I did not let the other boys see my tears.

Even though the Micawbers were poor, they often shared their own food with me and I was invited to sit with them around the fire when the nights were cold. Mr Micawber's debts increased. Creditors came

to the house at all hours and some of them were quite ferocious. In these wretched circumstances the Micawbers were forced to begin pawning their few, remaining possessions. Every day after work I would carry a rug, or a chair, or a small table, or some other item to the pawnbroker's shop and bring back just a few shillings. But Mr Micawber remained cheerful. His favourite expression was 'Something will turn up'.

In time, Mr Micawber's difficulties came to a crisis and, early one morning, he was arrested and taken to the King's Bench Prison where he would remain until his debts could be paid. His family was allowed to live with him so Mrs Micawber and the children moved into the prison too.

Mrs Micawber found me a cheap room that was close enough to the prison for me to visit them each evening after work.

On one of these visits, some six weeks

later, Mr Micawber told me that a rich relative had died in Australia and left him enough money to pay off his debts. He was to be released the following day and he and his family would travel to Plymouth to start a new life. Next morning I met the whole family at the coach station. I was sad to see them leave for I had become very fond of them.

With the Micawbers gone, I was lonelier than ever, so I decided to run away. I would try to find the only relative I had in the world, my aunt, Miss Betsey. As I didn't know where she lived, I wrote a letter to Peggotty and asked her where my aunt lived. I soon received Peggotty's answer. She told me that Miss Betsey lived at Dover and that the enclosed half-guinea was to get me there.

I hired a cart to take me to Dover but the driver took my half-guinea and my small box of clothes and drove off without me. I ran after him as fast as I could but I lost him and was left panting and crying in the muddy street. I had a few shillings left from my week's pay but it was not sufficient for my fare to Dover, so I set forth on foot. At night, I slept out in the fields, under hedges or haystacks, and trudged on miserably during the day. My money was soon gone and I had to pawn most of the clothes I was wearing to buy food. By the time I reached Dover I had been walking for six days. My shoes were worn through, my clothes were in rags and my hair was uncombed and dirty.

I must have been a pitiful sight for a kindly carriage-driver gave me a penny when he directed me to Miss Betsey Trotwood's house – a very neat, little cottage with bow-windows that looked out over the sea.

I was afraid to approach the cottage because I looked such a wretched sight. I waited at the gate until the door opened. A

tall, slim lady with grey hair appeared. She wore gardening gloves and she had a pruning knife in her hand and she noticed me at once.

"Go away! No boys here! They are not allowed!" she cried.

"If you please, Aunt Betsey, I am your nephew," I said, walking timidly towards her.

"Oh, Lord!" she exclaimed and sat flat down in the garden path. I spoke again.

"I am David Copperfield, of Blunderstone, in Suffolk. You were there on the night I was born and saw my dear mother. I have been neglected and ill-treated since she died, so I ran away to you. A thief took my money and I have never slept in a bed since I began walking from London six days ago."

Then, overcome by weariness and despair, I began to cry miserably.

My aunt got up in a great hurry and took me into the house. She gave me something

to drink and put me on the sofa with a shawl under my head. After a time she called out,

"Mr Dick, I wish to speak to you. Please come in here."

A pleasant-looking gentleman with grey hair came into the parlour. His eyes had a strange, distant brightness in them and, although he seemed childish in his ways, he had a friendly smile.

"I need your advice, Mr Dick," said my aunt. "You have heard me mention my late nephew, David Copperfield. Well, this is his son, young David Copperfield. He has run away and come to me. What shall I do with him?"

"Why, if I was you," said Mr Dick, "I should . . . wash him! . . . and then feed him!"

When I had bathed, they dressed me in a shirt and a pair of trousers belonging to Mr Dick and tied me up in two or three

large shawls. I cannot judge what sort of a bundle I looked like but I felt a very hot one indeed. I soon lay on the sofa again and fell asleep.

On waking several hours later I told my aunt about my poor mother's miserable marriage to Mr Murdstone. I also told her of the harsh and cruel treatment I had received from him. When I had finished my story my aunt said,

"Oh, that cruel man! I cannot imagine what possessed that poor, unfortunate girl to marry him."

After breakfast the next day my aunt informed me that she had written a letter to Mr Murdstone. I was very alarmed.

"Does he know where I am, Aunt?" I said anxiously.

"Yes," she replied, "I have told him."

"Shall I have to go back? I don't know

what I shall do if I have to go back to Mr Murdstone!" I cried.

"I don't know," said my aunt. "We shall see."

Then my aunt brought out her work-box and sat down to work. After a short while she spoke again.

"I would like you to go upstairs and give my regards to Mr Dick," she said, "and tell him I would be pleased to know how he is getting on with his Memorial."

Upstairs, I found Mr Dick working on his book – a Memorial to the Lord Chancellor about his affairs. I later learned from my aunt that he had been writing it for ten years. Apparently Mr Dick's harmless illness made it impossible for him to write more than a few pages without mentioning the beheading of King Charles the First.

I delivered my aunt's message.

"Ha!" said Mr Dick, laying down his pen.

"How does the world go? I shouldn't wish it to be mentioned, but it's a mad world, boy." Then he gave a strange kind of laugh and showed me his paper kite which must have been as much as seven feet high.

"What do you think of that for a kite?" he asked.

I told him that it was a beautiful one. Mr Dick smiled happily and said,

"I made it. One day we'll fly it, you and I."

We would have gone out to fly the great kite but I could not move around easily in the clothes I had been given to wear. I went downstairs to my aunt.

"Well, child," she said. "What do you think of him?"

"Is he . . . is Mr Dick out of his mind?" I stammered.

"No, indeed, he is not!" said my aunt. "He has been *called* mad. If it hadn't been for me, his own brother would have shut him up in an asylum for life. I considered him sane so I took him to live with me. For the past ten years Mr Dick has been my best friend and adviser."

The next few days passed quickly. My aunt, Miss Betsey, and Mr Dick were especially kind to me. The happy hours we spent together made me almost forget my miserable past.

Then one morning Mr and Miss Murdstone came to see my aunt. I was terrified.

"Shall I go upstairs, Aunt?" I asked, trembling.

"Certainly not!" she said and she pushed me into a corner near her. Then Mr Murdstone spoke.

"Miss Trotwood," he began, "this unhappy boy, David, has caused us a great deal of trouble and anxiety. He is obstinate and has a violent and uncontrollable temper."

"I agree entirely," said Miss Murdstone,

glaring at me. Mr Murdstone spoke again,

"Miss Trotwood," he said, "I am here to take him back. I shall deal with him as I see fit."

"Nonsense!" said my aunt. "I don't believe a word of it. Your shameful actions no doubt caused the death of this poor boy's mother. *You* ought to be severely punished for turning her son, a mere ten-year-old child, out to earn his own living while you and your spiteful sister lived in comfort in a house that rightly belongs to David. He suffered harm from being at your mercy. Nevertheless he must decide what he wants to do." Then she turned to me and said,

"What do you say, David? Are you ready to go back with them?"

"No, Aunt Betsey, no. Please don't let me go," I begged. "Neither Mr nor Miss Murdstone has ever liked me, or has ever been kind to me. They made my poor mother and Peggotty unhappy. They neglected me and made me miserable. Please don't let them take me back."

Mr Murdstone's face was white with rage.

"Miss Trotwood," he sàid angrily, "I am here either to take the boy back and to deal with him as I choose, or to leave him in your care. I will have nothing more to do with him if he remains here with you."

"Mr Dick," said my aunt, "what shall I do with this child?"

Mr Dick considered, hesitated, brightened, then answered,

"Have him measured for a suit of clothes immediately."

"Mr Dick, thank you, your common sense is invaluable," said my aunt joyfully. Then she turned to the Murdstones and said,

"Good day, sir, and good-bye! Good day to you, ma'am. If you come to my door again I'll knock you down and tread on you!"

Miss Murdstone and her brother walked out of the house and I ran and threw my arms around Aunt Betsey's neck. I kissed her and thanked her and I thanked Mr Dick too. He agreed to become my guardian, jointly with my aunt. So I began my new life, with not only two wonderful, new guardians but also with a new name, for Aunt Betsey decided to call me Trotwood Copperfield.

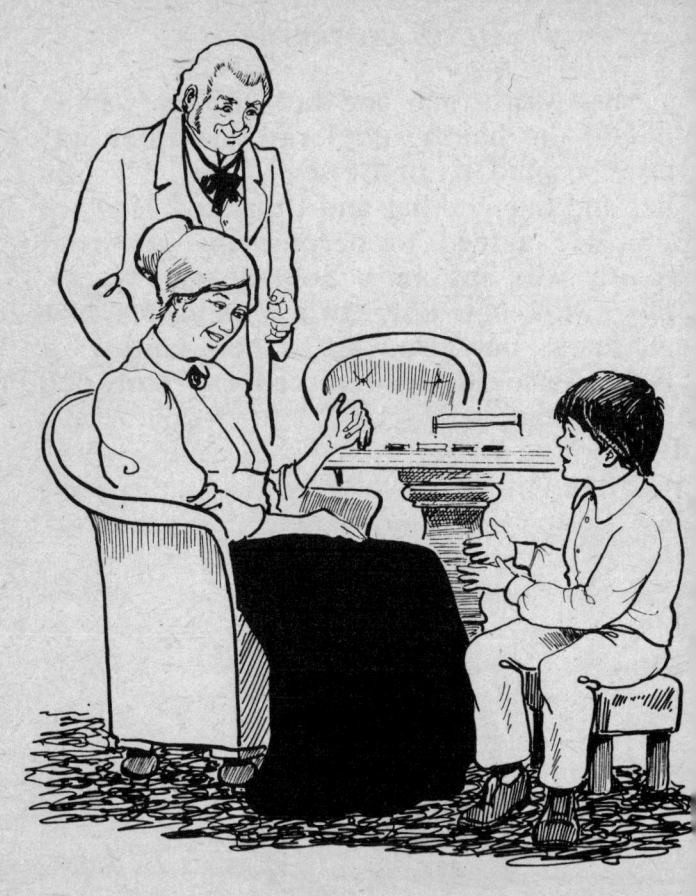

## Chapter 6
### I Start a New Life

For the next few weeks my aunt and Mr Dick were very kind to me and I soon recovered from all my suffering. Aunt Betsey had shortened my adopted name of Trotwood into Trot.

"Trot," she said one evening as she and Mr Dick were playing backgammon, "we must not forget your education. Would you like to go to school at Canterbury?"

I replied that as it was so near to her I would like it very much. A cart was ordered for the next morning and we set off at ten

o'clock for the ride to Canterbury. As she drove along my aunt told me that we were going to see her lawyer, Mr Wickfield, to seek his advice as to which would be a suitable school for me. In time we came to a very old house and my aunt stopped the cart at the door. The whole house seemed to be leaning towards the road and I noticed a gaunt, white face appear at a window on the ground floor and quickly disappear. Then the door was opened and I saw that the face belonged to a thin, red-haired boy of fifteen, but looking years older. He was dressed all in black. He had hardly any eyebrows, no eyelashes and his hands were long and bony.

"Is Mr Wickfield at home, Uriah Heep?" Aunt Betsey asked.

"Yes, Mr Wickfield's at home, ma'am," said the boy. "He is in his office. Please come in."

Mr Wickfield came out of his office to

greet us. He was a handsome, old gentleman with white hair and black eyebrows. He smiled at my aunt and said,

"Well, Miss Trotwood, what brings you here? Not trouble, I hope?"

"No," she replied. "This is my nephew, Trotwood Copperfield. I have brought him here to put him into a good school – a school where he will be well taught and well treated. Kindly advise me as to which would be the best school for him."

Mr Wickfield recommended Doctor Strong's School for Boys. It was not a boarding school so Mr Wickfield suggested I live in his home during the week and at Aunt Betsey's at the weekends. My aunt was pleased with the arrangements made for me and she soon left for home.

Then Mr Wickfield introduced me to his little housekeeper – his daughter Agnes – who was a delightfully cheerful girl of about my own age. She showed me up to my room; a glorious, old room that seemed as bright and cheerful as Agnes herself.

After dinner that evening I saw Uriah Heep closing up the office. I went in and shook hands with him. But what a clammy hand his was! When he had gone I rubbed my hand to get rid of his touch for something about him made me very uneasy.

Next morning I entered on school life again. I went to the school with Mr Wickfield and was introduced to my new master, Doctor Strong, a man in his sixties, and a very pretty, young lady whom he called Annie. I was most surprised to hear Mr Wickfield address her as Mrs Strong, for I had assumed that she was the Doctor's daughter.

Doctor Strong was compiling a new Dictionary in his free time. Adams, our head-boy, had calculated that at the rate the

Doctor was going it would take one thousand six hundred and forty-nine years to complete!

I was happy at Doctor Strong's school for it was an excellent one, as different from Mr Creakle's as good is from evil. Doctor Strong was kind to all his boys. He was a very good teacher whom we all loved and respected and we learned our lessons well.

My happiness was marred only by the ever-chilling presence of Uriah Heep.

## Chapter 7
## I Visit Old Friends

My life was happy as I progressed from childhood up to youth. I was now seventeen and the head-boy at school. Doctor Strong referred to me in public as a promising, young scholar. Agnes Wickfield, now a graceful, young woman, was my friend and counsellor. I told her everything – I told her of school; of my loves and my fights; of my hopes and dreams.

When my school-days drew to an end my aunt and I had many earnest discussions about my future occupation. I had no par-

ticular leaning towards any one career so my aunt suggested a month's change of scene to give me time to reach a positive decision.

"Trot, my dear," she said, "I think you should go to Yarmouth to see Peggotty and on the way back you could spend a few days in London."

"Thank you, Aunt Betsey, I should like that very much," I replied.

Before setting off for Yarmouth I went to Canterbury to say good-bye to Agnes and to her father, Mr Wickfield, who had aged considerably in the short time since I had seen him last. His eyes had a wild look in them, his hands trembled and his speech was slurred. Agnes was very worried about this change in her father. Indeed, she seemed almost terrified by it.

My parting from Agnes was hard to bear. Heavy at heart, I packed up my books and clothes to be sent to Dover. Uriah Heep

was so eager to help me with my boxes that I thought he was more than glad to see me go.

I took my seat on the London coach. It was interesting to be sitting there; well-educated, well-dressed and with plenty of money in my pocket and to look out for the places where I had slept on that dreadful journey to my aunt more than seven years ago.

The coach made an overnight stop at an inn at Charing Cross. I went and sat by the coffee-room fire after dinner and was soon deep in thought about my future. When at last I rose to go to bed I caught a glimpse of a handsome, well-dressed, young man standing by the door. I knew him in an instant.

"Steerforth!" I called out. "Steerforth! Won't you speak to me?"

He turned and stared at me.

"My God!" he suddenly exclaimed. "It's little Copperfield!"

So great was my happiness at seeing my old school friend that I would have hugged him and wept for joy had I not been a well-educated, young gentleman. I brushed away the few tears that I had not been able to keep back and then we sat down together, side by side, and talked about the past years. I told him of everything that had happened in my life since the day I left Salem House and he told me all that happened to him during the same time. I learned that he was now on the way home to visit his mother having completed his studies at Oxford University.

I told him that I was on the way to Yarmouth to see my old nurse, Peggotty, and her family. I also told him that my aunt had given me a month to decide upon a career.

"Why don't you come with me?" I said. "We could have a most enjoyable visit."

"A splendid idea!" said Steerforth. "And as you are in no hurry, you must first come home with me to Highgate for a day or two."

I accepted his invitation and we left for Highgate the following day. When we arrived I was introduced to Mrs Steerforth, an elderly lady who had a proud manner and a handsome face. I also met her companion, Miss Rosa Dartle, an overly-thin, young lady with dark eyes, dark hair and a scar on her lip. To my surprise, Steerforth told me that he was to blame for her scar.

"I did that when I was a young boy. She made me angry and I threw a hammer at her. What a young angel I must have been! But she loves me still," he said with a laugh that made me feel uneasy.

The next day I met Steerforth's servant, a respectable–looking man named Littimer,

who had first worked for Steerforth at the University. During my visit he waited on the two of us. He brought horses for us and Steerforth gave me lessons in riding; he brought foils and Steerforth gave me fencing lessons; he brought gloves when Steerforth gave me lessons in boxing.

The days passed quickly and at the end of a week Steerforth and I travelled down to Yarmouth. We spent the night at an inn and breakfasted late in the morning. Steerforth had been out strolling about the beach before I was up.

"Well, young Copperfield," he said cheerfully, "I've already met most of the boatmen in the town and I'm sure I've seen the boat 'house' you described where Mr Peggotty lives. In fact I nearly decided to go in and announce myself as David Copperfield, grown beyond all recognition. But as you see, I didn't, and now you must go and see

your old nurse to be cried over for a couple of hours. I will meet you there later."

I gave him directions for finding Mr Barkis's cottage and went on alone to see Peggotty. I had written to her regularly but it was now more than seven years since we had seen each other. Peggotty came to the door in answer to my knock but she did not recognise me.

"What is your business here, sir?" she asked respectfully. I tried to disguise my voice by speaking in a gruff manner.

"I'm seeking information about the Copperfield house in Blunderstone," I said.

Peggotty took a step backward and put her hands to her face.

"Peggotty! My dear Peggotty!" I cried to her.

"My darling boy!" she cried, and we both burst into tears and were locked in each other's arms.

Although Barkis was ill in bed with rheumatism he greeted me with absolute enthusiasm and we talked for hours about the times past when I had delivered his 'Barkis is willin'!' messages to Peggotty.

I told Peggotty about Steerforth and when he arrived a short time later she was soon completely won over by his easy charm and good looks. We left at eight o'clock to visit Mr Peggotty, Ham and Emily. When we reached the boat 'house' I lifted the latch and we walked softly into the room.

I saw at once the look of joy on Mr Peggotty's face. Seated comfortably by the fire, he was listening intently to Ham and Emily who were holding hands and talking to him about something – something that had Mrs Gummidge clapping her hands in a fever of excitement.

Emily saw us first, then Ham.

"Mas'r Davy! It's Mas'r Davy!" he shouted,

and in an instant we were all shaking hands with one another and laughing and talking non-stop. We soon learned that Emily and Ham were to be married. We congratulated them and then Steerforth entertained us with stories that kept us laughing and talking for hours. At first Emily was very shy but when she found how considerately Steerforth spoke to her she happily joined in our conversation.

It was almost midnight when we left. Steerforth had enjoyed meeting the family and was obviously very taken with Emily but I was shocked by his unexpected and cold remark that Ham seemed too stupid a person for her to marry. Then I decided that Steerforth must be joking for I saw a mischievous twinkle in his eye as we walked back to the inn.

Steerforth and I spent more than two weeks in Yarmouth. Steerforth was a good sailor and whenever he and Mr Peggotty

went out boating together I revisited my childhood home at Blunderstone. Many changes had taken place; the Murdstones had moved away and the house was empty; half the windows were shut up and the garden had run wild. Overwhelmed with sadness, I lingered by the graves beneath the tree where my father and my mother and my tiny half-brother lay buried.

Late one evening, when I returned from my parting visit to Blunderstone, I found Steerforth alone in Mr Peggotty's house, staring thoughtfully at the fire. His face was dark and he seemed troubled. I spoke to him and when he looked up there was a smile on his face and his usual good humour had returned.

"I have bought a boat," he said cheerfully, "and Mr Peggotty will be the master of her while I'm away. She needs new sails so Littimer will come down to see it done and

to see her re-named. She's to be called the *Little Emily*."

I was surprised by his good news for Steerforth had looked so desolate as he sat by the fire.

Later that night I went to Peggotty's house where I met a young woman named Martha. She and Emily had been friends since they were children and Martha had come to seek Emily's help because she was in some kind of trouble. When Emily heard Martha's story she wept and then she gave the poor girl enough money to start a new life in London.

# Chapter 8
## I Choose an Occupation

Steerforth and I left Yarmouth the next morning. After saying good-bye to Peggotty and her family and all our friends we boarded the coach to London.

For some time we held no conversation for Steerforth was unusually silent and I was lost in thought as to my future. Eventually Steerforth said,

"Tell me, David, have you settled on a career?"

"I think I would like to be a proctor," I replied, for that was the career my

aunt had suggested to me in a recent letter.

Steerforth and I talked at length about proctors and that occupation and then we parted. He went home to Highgate and I went to the hotel in London where my aunt was staying.

"Well, Trot," said Aunt Betsey as she embraced me. "What do you think of the plan to become a proctor?"

"I like it very much," I replied, "but I am concerned that the proctor training might be too expensive."

"Trot, my child," she said gently as she took my hands in hers, "it is too late for regrets but perhaps I might have been better friends with your poor father when he was alive. And when you were a small child perhaps I might have been better friends with your poor mother, for the disappointment I felt at your being born David, rather than the Betsey I had hoped for, is long past. Then you came to me, Trot, and you have always been a credit and a pleasure to me. Your love has done more for me than ever this old woman did for you. Now, if I have any object in life, it is to provide for your being a good and happy man."

My aunt embraced me again and my eyes were wet with tears as I thanked her.

The next morning we went to the office of my aunt's proctors, Spenlow and Jorkins. My aunt had arranged for me to be taken on as a proctor-in-training for a trial period of one month. The terms of my employment were agreed and then Aunt Betsey and I went to see the furnished rooms she had found for me. The rooms were at the top of the house and had a fine view of the river.

It was a wonderfully fine thing to have that lofty castle to myself but there were times when I was lonely, particularly at night.

It was then that I thought of Agnes and of how much I missed her.

Then one morning I received a note from Agnes. She was in London with her father and Uriah Heep and she wanted to see me at her hotel that afternoon.

Agnes was sitting by the fire when I arrived and although she greeted me cheerfully, I knew something was worrying her. Then she told me that her father had taken Uriah Heep as a partner in his business and now she feared that Heep was taking advantage of her father for Mr Wickfield was old and weak and he seemed to be afraid of Uriah Heep.

I had never seen Agnes cry but she wept now and I did my best to comfort her. Later that evening when Agnes and her father had gone to bed Uriah Heep told me that he loved Agnes and he wanted to marry her. The thought of this wretch marrying Agnes

– my sweet Agnes – filled me with such rage that I had a powerful urge to seize the red-hot poker from the fireplace and run him through with it. Furthermore, I was suspicious of Heep's interest in the Wickfield business. I was uneasy in his company and returned to my rooms as soon as I could get away.

I was happy in my new employment and the time passed quickly. One day, Mr Spenlow invited me to spend a weekend at his home in the country. His daughter, Dora, met us at the door and from the moment I set eyes on her I was in love, for she was the loveliest creature on earth. We walked and talked for hours and that weekend was one of the happiest of my life.

On my return to London I went to dinner at a friend's house. To my surprise and delight one of the other guests was none other than Tommy Traddles, my old schoolfriend. How quickly my mind flew back to

my school days at Salem House when Tommy Traddles had been caned almost every day. We arranged to meet at his home the next day and he gave me the address of a house in Camden Town.

I soon found the street. It was a dirty, untidy, little street with piles of rotting vegetables lying in the gutter. The place was a powerful reminder to me of the days when I lived with Mr and Mrs Micawber.

Traddles was on the landing. He greeted me warmly and led me into his neat, little room. We talked about our school days at Mr Creakle's and about our lives since that time. Traddles had been orphaned as a child and had been brought up by an uncle. Soon after Traddles left school the uncle had died leaving nothing to Traddles in his will. Since then, Traddles had taken many odd jobs to support himself while studying to become a lawyer. Also, he was engaged to a curate's daughter but he couldn't marry his 'dearest girl', as he called her, until his financial circumstances improved.

"Our motto is 'Wait and Hope!'. I don't make much but I don't spend much," said Traddles. "I board with the people downstairs, who are very kind people indeed. Both Mr and Mrs Micawber have known hard times in life."

"The Micawbers!" I cried in surprise. "Why, I know them extremely well! I must go and see them at once."

At first, Mr and Mrs Micawber did not recognise me so I quickly introduced myself. They were really pleased to see me. We talked of old times and then I asked Traddles and the Micawbers to set a date for them to come and dine with me.

My three guests arrived at the appointed time. My little party was quite a success and I enjoyed entertaining my new-found, old friends. After they had gone I heard a quick step on the stairs and James Steerforth walked in!

He said he had just come from Yarmouth where he had spent the past week sailing in his boat. I asked him about my friends.

"Emily and Ham are not married yet," said Steerforth. "Mr Peggotty is well but Mr Barkis, the carriage driver, lies dangerously ill with a fever and may well be about to take his last journey."

"I must go to Peggotty," I said. "I will go down to Yarmouth early tomorrow morning."

Then, to my surprise, Steerforth invited me to go with him to Highgate first. He told me he was going to visit his mother whom he had not seen for a long time. Then he said,

"Say you'll come, Copperfield, for who knows when we may meet again, else?"

I agreed to go to Highgate with him but

I was puzzled by his strange remark. Mrs Steerforth's companion, Miss Dartle, met us at the door.

"I take it you are the one who is responsible for James's long absences from home," she said sharply, and I became even more puzzled.

"I have no knowledge of Steerforth's affairs," I said, "for I have not seen him for a long while, until last night."

Steerforth said nothing but I could see that he was troubled by something.

That night, before going to my room, I told Steerforth I would be gone before he woke in the morning. He put his hands on my shoulders and held me as if unwilling to let me go.

"David," he said, with a smile, "if anything should ever separate us, you must think of me at my best."

"You have no best to me, Steerforth,"

I replied, "and no worst. You will always be loved as my good and dear friend."

Then we shook hands and we parted.

## Chapter 9
## A Grievous Loss

I got down to Yarmouth in the evening and went to Peggotty's house. Mr Peggotty answered my low tap at the door and I followed him into the kitchen. Emily was sitting by the fire, silent and sad. Ham was standing near her but she seemed to shrink from his touch when he tried to comfort her.

As I sat counting the ticking of the clock I thought about Emily and Ham, who were to be married in a fortnight.

Then Peggotty came down. She took me

in her arms and begged me to come upstairs to the bedroom where Barkis lay dying.

"He's going out with the tide," said Mr Peggotty in a whisper. "Along the coast, people can't die unless the tide's nearly out."

We remained there, watching him. Hours later, he opened his eyes, tried to stretch out his arm and said to me with a faint smile,

"Barkis is willin'!"

And, it being time, he went out with the tide.

Before we parted after Barkis's funeral at Blunderstone, we all arranged to meet that night in Mr Peggotty's old boat 'house'. Ham would bring Emily and I would walk back at my leisure.

Rain was falling heavily by the time I reached the boat 'house' but there was a moon behind the clouds and it was not dark. Mr Peggotty greeted me and led me inside.

Peggotty and Mrs Gummidge were sitting by a bright fire.

A little while later Ham came in, alone.

"Wheer's Emily?" said Mr Peggotty.

Ham made a motion with his head, as if she were outside. Then he looked at me and said,

"Mas'r Davy, will you come out a minute and see what Emily and me has got to show you?"

We went out, and Ham closed the door behind us.

"She's gone! Emily's run away!" he said, and he wept, his face deathly pale. "What am I to say to Mr Peggotty? How can I tell him?"

Before I could speak, the door opened and Mr Peggotty came out. He saw the look of despair on Ham's face and he knew.

Emily had left a note. We went back inside and I read the note aloud to the others:

"'When you see this, I shall be far away. When I leave my home, it will be never to come back, unless he brings me back a lady. God bless all! My last tears, and thanks, for uncle!'"

"Who's the man?" said Mr Peggotty, in a low voice.

Ham glanced at me and suddenly I felt a shock, for I had guessed. I sank down in a chair.

"For some while past," Ham faltered, "there's been a servant, and his gen'lm'n, about here."

As Ham described Steerforth and Littimer, I felt Peggotty's arm round my neck but I could not have spoken or moved if the house had been about to fall down.

"Don't tell me his name's Steerforth!" cried Mr Peggotty.

"Mas'r Davy," said Ham in a broken voice, "it ain't no fault of yourn, but his name is Steerforth and he's a damned villain!"

Mr Peggotty was overcome with grief and vowed he would search the world to find his poor, lost niece. Then he broke down and cried and I cried too.

## Chapter 10
## I Fall on Hard Times

I returned to London with Peggotty. Taking the management of her affairs into my own hands, I proved Barkis's will and soon got everything in order.

A week later, Mr Spenlow invited me to Dora's birthday picnic. I was overjoyed. I bought flowers for Dora but when I presented my bouquet her little dog, Jip, growled and barked with jealousy. I was happy with Dora and, four days later, we were engaged but we agreed to keep it a secret from Mr Spenlow for a time. I did, however, tell

Peggotty on my return to London and I also wrote and told Agnes.

One day, when Peggotty and I returned to my rooms, I was amazed to find, of all people on earth, my aunt and Mr Dick! She was sitting on her luggage drinking tea, with her cat on her lap and her two birds in a cage by her side. Mr Dick, with more luggage piled about him, was leaning thoughtfully on a great kite.

"My dear Aunt! What an unexpected pleasure!" I cried, and then I waited for her to speak.

"Trot," she said, as she finished her tea, "why do you think I choose to sit here on my luggage?"

Unable to guess, I merely shook my head.

"Because I'm ruined, my dear!" said Aunt Betsey, "Dick knows it. All I have in the world is in this room, except the cottage and that is now let. But we must overcome misfortune, my dear Trot, and you must be firm and self-reliant."

I could hardly have received a greater shock.

"And now, Trot," my aunt said calmly, "we must find a bed for Dick tonight and, to save further expense, perhaps you can make up a bed here for me as it's only for tonight."

As soon as I was able to think clearly again, I took Mr Dick to a rooming house and soon had him settled for the night. When I got back to my rooms, Aunt Betsey was pacing up and down. She and Peggotty had been discussing my engagement.

"Oh, Trot!" she said. "So you fancy yourself in love?"

"Fancy, Aunt! Indeed I adore her with my whole soul!" I exclaimed. "I know we are young and some may think us foolish but we love one another."

"Trot, my dear, it may come to nothing. But there's time enough for it to come to something one day," Aunt Betsey said affectionately.

I was grateful for her words of encouragement but I could not sleep that night. I thought about my being poor – I was earning nothing during my proctor training – and I wondered miserably if Mr Spenlow would permit Dora to marry me. In my poor circumstances how would I pay court to Dora and assist my aunt also?

The next day I informed Mr Spenlow and his partner, Mr Jorkins, of my reduced circumstances. However, when I told them that I would have to cancel my training, they refused to return my aunt's thousand pounds – the money advanced to them for my training.

Despair seized me as I left the office and started for home. As I walked along the

street, trying to come to terms with my uncertain future, a hansom cab came to a stop at my feet, causing me to look up.

"Agnes!" I cried joyfully. "Of all the people in the world I would wish to see at this moment, you are the one!"

She took my arm as she stepped from the cab and we walked on together. Agnes had come to London to see my aunt, having learned of her financial difficulties, for they had become close friends over the years. Agnes had not come alone; her father and Uriah Heep were with her. Uriah Heep had become a partner in Mr Wickfield's business and now lived in their house.

"I cannot be as close to Papa as I would wish," Agnes said sadly, "and I'm sure Heep is planning some fraud or treachery against him."

I felt Agnes's arm tremble in mine as I led her to my rooms. Aunt Betsey greeted

her warmly and we began to talk about my
aunt's misfortune. It seems she had been
advised by the firm of Wickfield and
Heep to invest in some bank stock.
Unfortunately, the bank failed and my aunt
lost everything.

"Oh, Aunt!" I wailed. "I must do
something!"

"Go to sea, do you mean?" said my aunt,
alarmed. "Or be a soldier? I won't hear of
it. You will finish your training and become
a proctor just as we planned."

Then Agnes turned to me and said,

"You must go ahead with your studies,
Trot, but perhaps you could work in your
free time. Doctor Strong, who now lives in
London, has asked Papa to find him a
secretary. I'm sure he would be pleased to
have his favourite, old pupil to help him on
the Dictionary he is still writing."

"Dear Agnes! What would I do without

you?" I said gratefully. "You are always my good angel."

"You already have your good angel, Dora," she said with a cheerful laugh.

I wrote to Doctor Strong and made an appointment for the next day. When I arrived he was walking in his garden.

"Why, my dear Copperfield, you are a man!" he said with a smile and we talked of old times. Then we discussed my proposal.

"Copperfield," said the Doctor, "I would be glad to have you as my secretary but don't you think you could do better with your qualifications? I can only afford to pay seventy pounds a year."

"It would double our income, Doctor Strong," I said. "I could work for you in my free time in the mornings and evenings and continue my proctor training during the day."

"Then so be it," said Doctor Strong, and

we settled my hours of work – two hours every morning and two or three hours every night, except on Saturdays and Sundays, which were to be my rest days.

I was busy now; up at five in the morning, and home at nine or ten at night. Mr Dick, however, had begun to fret and worry because there was nothing useful he could do to help Aunt Betsey. I went to see my old friend Traddles who, on hearing of Mr Dick's extraordinarily neat handwriting, employed him to copy legal documents. Traddles then told me that I could get a job reporting the debates in Parliament for the newspapers, if I could master shorthand.

Before I left, Traddles handed me a letter from our old friend, Mr Micawber. Traddles had been lending him money over a period of time and Mr Micawber had written to say that he had moved to Canterbury and was now working as a confidential clerk to Uriah Heep.

The very thought of Heep disturbed me for I did not trust him.

## Chapter 11
## Dora

As the days passed, Aunt Betsey and Peggotty became the best of friends. But the time had come for Peggotty to return home. There had been no news of her brother since the day he had left Yarmouth in search of his beloved Emily and now Peggotty felt it was her duty to care for Ham.

Before she left on the coach to Yarmouth, Peggotty made me promise that I would go to her if I needed money at any time.

That evening I went to see Dora and asked her if she could love a beggar, because that

was what I had become. Dora simply laughed and shook her curls. I was enchanted by her childish ways.

"Dora, my dearest," I cried, "though I am your ruined David, is your heart still mine?"

"Oh, yes! But I don't want to hear any more talk of being poor and working hard!" said Dora.

I loved my dear, sweet Dora and I went on loving her completely but I realised that she would always be unable to face the realities of life.

Each night, after I came home from the Doctor's, I practised my shorthand for the Parliamentary debates. It was like learning a new alphabet and my dreams were of curves and marks like flies' legs.

Then one day I received another great shock; Mr Spenlow was killed in a fall from his horse and Dora went to live in Putney

with her two maiden aunts. I saw nothing of Dora now and I soon became depressed. Aunt Betsey asked me to go to Dover to see that all was well at her cottage, which was still let. I found everything in satisfactory order at the cottage and I decided to visit Agnes and Mr Wickfield in Canterbury before returning to London. I had no opportunity to talk to Agnes alone during my first afternoon and Uriah Heep's ominous presence seemed to hang over the house like a dark cloud. That evening the men were left alone after dinner. Heep urged Mr Wickfield to drink several glasses of wine then he suddenly said,

"I've an ambition to make your Agnes my Agnes, Mr Wickfield! I'm an 'umble individual but to be her 'usband . . ."

Agnes's father rose from the table with a savage cry and seemed to go mad for the moment, tearing out his hair, beating his

head, his face distorted and his eyes staring wildly. I put my arms round him and steadied him. Then Mr Wickfield pointed at Heep and cried,

"Look at my torturer. He has ruined my good name and reputation. He has destroyed my peace and quiet and he has taken my house and home but he will never marry my Agnes. Never! Never!" and he sank into a chair and sobbed.

A moment later Agnes glided into the room and gently guided her father upstairs to bed.

"He's had too much wine," said Heep. "He'll think better of my proposal when tomorrow comes."

I made no reply and Heep left the room. Agnes joined me a while later. She had been weeping but her face was calm and beautiful. I took her hand in mine and said,

"Dear Agnes, I speak as a friend who

loves you very much. You are too good for a man like Uriah Heep and you must not marry him, not for any reason at all."

"I must put my trust in God," said Agnes with a wan smile. And then, moments later, she slipped out of the room.

On my return to London I wrote to Dora's aunts and obtained their permission to visit Dora on Saturdays and Sundays. My work and my studies kept me busy through the week and my weekend visits with Dora were wonderful times for me. I was, however, troubled by one thing; Dora was spoiled by too much attention. Her aunts curled her hair and made pretty trinkets for her. Dora was happy but I did not think that treating her like a plaything would prepare her for married life.

Then, to my surprise, Dora asked me to give her a cookery-book and to show her how to keep household accounts. But the cookery-book made her head ache and the numbers made her cry when she couldn't make them add up, so the books were put in the corner of the room. Dora soon trained Jip to stand on them and she was so delighted at this that I was very glad I had bought the books.

## Chapter 12
## A Chance Meeting with Mr Peggotty

One snowy night I left work at Doctor Strong's to walk the shortest way home through St Martin's Lane. I saw, at the corner, a woman's face. It stared at mine and then disappeared down a narrow lane. I knew that face. It was Emily's friend, Martha Endell; the woman to whom Emily had given the money that night in Peggotty's kitchen all those months ago. I walked on towards St Martin's Church where I saw a man place a bundle on the steps and stoop to adjust it. As I approached, he stood up,

turned and we stared at each other. I was face to face with Mr Peggotty! We shook hands heartily, neither of us able to speak at first. Then Mr Peggotty gripped me tight and said,

"Mas'r Davy! It does my heart good to see you, sir."

"And mine to see you, my dear old friend!" I replied. "Come, we must get out of the cold." I took his arm and led him to a nearby inn.

When I saw him in the light, I noticed that he was greyer and the lines in his face were deeper. He told me of his continuing search for Emily. He had already followed her on foot through France and Italy and over the mountains of Switzerland. It seems Emily had been sending money to Mrs Gummidge for her uncle but, as she never gave an address, Mr Peggotty had been searching the places where Emily's letters

were postmarked. Her last letter had come from Germany and Mr Peggotty was on his way there now. Sadly, he showed me Emily's letters and the money which he had not touched. As he spoke, the door opened a little and the snow drifted in. I saw Martha at the door and I saw her careworn face. She was listening intently. I said nothing of her presence to Mr Peggotty because I knew he disapproved of the friendship between Martha and Emily. I asked him about Ham. Mr Peggotty shook his head.

"Ham never complains," he said. "He works hard but he is deeply hurt by this business."

Mr Peggotty placed his bundle of letters carefully in his breast pocket and rose to go. I glanced up and saw that Martha was gone from the door. When I left the inn I saw no footprints for the snow had already covered them. Even my new tracks began to die away in the fast-falling snow as I made my way home.

## Chapter 13
## Uriah Heep

Agnes and her father came to stay with Doctor Strong for two weeks. The visit had been arranged because Agnes thought it would be good for her father to spend some time with his old friend, the Doctor. Uriah Heep came too.

Late one night I saw a light in the Doctor's study. I went in to bid him good night and was surprised to find Uriah Heep and Mr Wickfield there with him. Mr Wickfield seemed deeply troubled and Doctor Strong was slumped in his chair, covering his face

with his hands. Before I could ask what had happened I heard Uriah Heep's voice.

"I felt it my duty," he said, "to tell Doctor Strong of his wife's close association with another man."

I was shocked and angered by Heep's cruel lie but I knew that the Doctor would believe it to be true because Annie, his beautiful wife, was many years younger than he. The evil Uriah Heep was a wicked liar and a cheat who seemed determined to destroy everyone's happiness by his villainous ways. I could hardly control my rage.

"And to think, Mr Wickfield," Heep continued, "that your Agnes and Mrs Strong have been such close friends! And as for Copperfield, surely he must have seen the goings-on when he has been working here with Doctor Strong these past weeks."

"You wretched villain!" I roared. "Do not involve me in your wickedness!" And I

truck his cheek with such force that my fingers burned. Still in a towering rage, I yelled,

"You may go to the devil!" Then I went quickly from the room.

I soon observed a change in the Doctor's household. The house was quiet now for Annie sat silent and tearful and Doctor Strong seemed to look older and sadder as the weeks passed. Their unhappiness was relieved only by Mr Dick's frequent visits. Walking up and down the garden with the Doctor and talking to Mrs Strong as he helped her to trim her favourite flowers, he became, in time, what no one else could be – a link between them.

During the time the Wickfields were visiting the Doctor I received a letter from Mrs Micawber which set me thinking.

'Mr Micawber,' she wrote, 'is entirely changed. He, who was once a caring father

to his children and a devoted husband to me, has grown secretive and distant. His manner has become cold and severe. This unhappy situation is hard to bear and I would welcome your advice.'

I was reluctant to offer any advice to a wife of Mrs Micawber's experience and could recommend only that she try to win back her husband by patience and kindness.

## Chapter 14
## Life with Dora

Weeks, months and seasons passed. I married my dear, little Dora when I reached the legal age of twenty-one.

I doubt whether two young birds could have known less about keeping house than my pretty Dora and I.

I engaged a servant to keep house for us but Dora couldn't bring herself to supervise the woman or to scold her when our meals were late or not served at all. It was an awful time for us. So, to avoid any arguments with my beloved Dora, I took charge of all

the household tasks myself. Dora was happy to spend her days playing with Jip but I was worried about her childish ways and went to Aunt Betsey for advice.

"Trot," she said kindly, "you must have patience for these are early days. You have chosen to marry a very pretty and a very affectionate girl. Your future is between you two. In a marriage you must sort your problems out yourselves."

I thanked my aunt for her good advice and Dora and I went on with our life together much as before. My work and my studies kept me busy. In my spare time in the evenings I wrote stories for a magazine, the income from my stories enabling me to give up my work with Doctor Strong.

Dora was bright and cheerful but she was not strong. As the months wore on, she grew weaker and she no longer danced around Jip. I began to carry her upstairs each night

and downstairs each morning. My aunt, the best and most cheerful of nurses, bustled around us with heaps of shawls and pillows. But, sometimes, when I lifted Dora up and she felt lighter in my arms, an empty feeling came upon me that filled me with fear.

## Chapter 15
## Mr Dick: A Very Remarkable Man

Although it had been some weeks since I had worked for the Doctor, I saw him frequently for we lived in his neighbourhood. Doctor Strong had become more depressed than ever over Uriah Heep's malicious lie.

One evening, Mr Dick came to see me.

"Trotwood," he said, "could you speak to me?"

"Why, certainly, Mr Dick," I replied. "Come in."

"Now, boy, I'm going to put a question

to you. What do you think of me in this respect?" he said, touching his forehead.

Before I could answer, he spoke again.

"I am simple and weak-minded, Trotwood. Your aunt pretends I am not but, I know I am. I would have been locked up years ago if she hadn't been my friend and taken care of me."

Then, laying one hand upon my knee, he said anxiously,

"I have seen clouds, sir – clouds between the Doctor and his beautiful wife."

I explained the situation and Uriah Heep's part in it, as simply as I could.

"Why has Miss Betsey, the most wonderful woman in the world, done nothing to set things right? And, a fine scholar like you, why have you done nothing?" said Mr Dick.

"It's too delicate and difficult a subject for us to interfere," I replied.

"Then, sir, I'll bring them together," he

cried. "I'm only a poor, simple fellow and they wouldn't blame me for interfering. After all, I'm only Mr Dick and Mr Dick is a nobody. I've been thinking about it for a while and I now have a plan. Yes, I have a plan!"

Two weeks passed and I had heard nothing more of Mr Dick's plan. I was beginning to think that in his unsettled state of mind he had either forgotten or abandoned the whole idea.

Then one evening when my aunt and I were visiting the Doctor, Mr Dick led Annie into the study. She fell to her knees at the Doctor's feet and said tearfully,

"Oh, my husband, I implore you to break this long silence. Tell me what it is that has come between us."

"Annie," said the Doctor, gently taking her hand. "My dear Annie. If there has been a change in our lives, the fault is mine.

There is no change in my affection and admiration for I truly love and honour you."

"I know in my heart that something is wrong," Annie sobbed. "If you will not tell me, then let one of your friends here speak."

There was a long silence. Then I reluctantly told her of Uriah Heep's scandalous lie.

Annie remained silent for a few moments then she took the Doctor's hand and kissed it.

"My dear husband," she said softly, "in my childhood I loved you as a father. Your wish to marry me came as a surprise, but I was proud to become your wife. Since then I have loved you as a dear and gentle husband and I have never wronged you."

"Annie, my dear, dear wife!" said the Doctor. He took her in his arms, mingling his grey hair with her dark brown curls.

We watched in silence, then my aunt walked over to Mr Dick and kissed him.

"You are a very remarkable man, Dick!" she said, "and never pretend to be anything else for I know better!"

Then we three stole quietly out of the study and went home.

# Chapter 16
## Immersed in Mystery

Walking home one evening after a solitary walk, I passed Mrs Steerforth's house. A maid came out and spoke to me.

"Mrs Steerforth wishes to speak to you, sir."

When I entered the parlour Mrs Steerforth said angrily,

"Has that girl, Emily, been found?"

I was quite astonished.

"No," I replied, "I thought she was with James."

"She has run away from him," she said

with a laugh. "If she is not found, perhaps she never will be! She may even be dead!"

"I beg you to tell me what you know of Emily," I said.

So Mrs Steerforth told me of Emily's travels through Europe with Steerforth and his servant, Littimer. It seems Emily had learned to speak several languages and was much admired wherever they went. But Steerforth had soon tired of her. He had left her in Italy with the suggestion that she marry Littimer, a man of her own station in life. Cast aside by Steerforth, Emily had become so violent that she had to be locked in her room. But she escaped through a window and had not been heard of since. Meanwhile, Steerforth was sailing the Spanish coast.

"Mrs Steerforth," I said coldly, "knowing all this, what is it that you want of me?"

"Why, to see if you knew where that

worthless girl is, of course. My dear son must have nothing more to do with her!" she replied.

I concealed my anger as best I could and said respectfully,

"Having known Emily's family since childhood, I can assure you, madam, that she would rather die than take anything from your son's hand now."

Then I left as quickly as I could. On the following evening I went to London in search of Mr Peggotty. Although he was always wandering about from place to place, I had seen him combing the streets of London for Emily. I found him in his room and gave him the news.

"My Emily's alive, Mas'r Davy, I know she is!" he said firmly.

"And if she should come to London," I said, "I believe she will try to find her friend Martha, the girl she helped before she left home."

"I think I know where to look for Martha, Mas'r Davy, for I have seen her in the street," said Mr Peggotty.

We were not far from Blackfriars Bridge when he turned his head and pointed to a lonely figure walking along the street. It was Martha. She turned down a street which led to the river and we went after her. It was a desolate place with discarded wheels, pipes, rusty iron steam boilers and other strange objects scattered all around. The girl we had followed moved slowly to the river's edge and stood looking at the water. Believing that she intended to drown herself, I rushed forward and seized her arm.

"No! Martha, no!" I cried.

She let out a terrified scream and struggled with me. Then Mr Peggotty grasped her other arm and we carried her to safety. When Martha finally recognised us, I told her about Emily.

"Martha," said Mr Peggotty, "Mas'r Davy and I believe Emily will come to London. Please help us to find her."

Martha lifted up her eyes and vowed that she would devote herself to the task of finding Emily. Then I gave her our two addresses and we parted.

Some days later Traddles and I received letters from the Micawbers which were both puzzling and alarming. Then to our surprise, Mr Micawber arrived, his face gloomy and his manner downcast.

"Gentlemen!" cried Mr Micawber. "You are friends in need, and friends indeed. You see before you a broken man. My mind is in turmoil and my self-respect is gone. My life is in ruins and the cause of it all is the deception, fraud and conspiracy of that atrocious villain . . . HEEP!"

I tried to calm him but he wouldn't hear a word.

"The struggle is over!" he raved. "I will lead this life no longer. I have been under a spell in that infernal scoundrel's service. I will not rest until I have blown to fragments that detestable serpent . . HEEP! I will live nowhere until I have choked the eyes out of the head of that cheat and liar . . . HEEP! I will expose that intolerable ruffian, that doomed traitor . . . HEEP!"

With that, he sank into a chair and looked at Aunt Betsey, Traddles, Mr Dick and me.

He asked us to meet him at a hotel in Canterbury the following week. He would then deliver the proof that would unmask Heep.

Then Mr Micawber rushed out of the house.

## Chapter 17
## A Dream Come True

Some months had passed since the night Mr Peggotty and I had spoken with Martha on the river bank. There had been no news yet of Emily but Mr Peggotty's determination and hope remained strong.

Then one evening, as I was walking alone in the garden, Martha arrived at the gate. She whispered anxiously,

"Can you come with me? I've been to Mr Peggotty's but he's not at home. I wrote down where he was to come and left it on his table. Can you come at once?"

We left immediately and turned towards London. I stopped a passing coach and we got into it. Martha gave the driver the address and then stayed silent until we reached Golden Square, which was now a much neglected area for the large houses had long since become poor lodgings let off in rooms. Martha stopped at one of these lodgings and beckoned me to follow her up the stairs. We climbed to the topmost floor and stood to catch our breath. I heard a distant footstep on the stairs. Then Mr Peggotty appeared and rushed into the room.

"Uncle!" cried Emily. A fearful cry followed the word. When I looked in I saw Mr Peggotty nursing the unconscious Emily in his arms.

"Mas'r Davy," he whispered in a trembling voice, "I thank my Heavenly Father for my dream has come true!"

Then he carried his motionless niece down the stairs.

The next day, Mr Peggotty came to see me when I was in the garden with my aunt. He told us of Emily's flight from Steerforth's servant, Littimer, and of how she had been befriended and hidden by a young woman who lived near them on the beach.

"Then," he continued, "my Emily became ill with fever but the woman cared for her until she was strong again. Emily gave the kind woman what little money she had and left for London."

Mr Peggotty wiped away the tears that had filled his eyes.

"And all the while," he said sadly, "my Emily was fearing to see me. But, by working at inns in Italy and France, she earned her passage to England. When Martha found her in London she told her how I still loved her and now Emily and me will never be parted."

My aunt was sobbing but I remained silent for a while. Then I said to Mr Peggotty,

"What are your plans for the future, good friend?"

"Emily and I will begin a new life in Australia," he replied. "We will sail as soon as I can take my farewell leave of Yarmouth. Perhaps, Mas'r Davy, you could do me the kind favour of going down with me to help me settle my affairs."

I readily agreed to accompany him for Dora was in good spirits and Aunt Betsey would stay with her.

I took a stroll about the town while Mr Peggotty revealed his plans to Ham and Peggotty. On my return, I helped Mr Peggotty settle his affairs. His fishing boat was disposed of and all his goods and furniture were sent to London docks for shipment to Australia. Now the doors of the boat 'house' stood open.

As I took a last look at my old bedroom, I thought of the days when Emily and I had played happily on the beach. Then I thought of Steerforth and a strange and foolish fear came over me – a fear that he was very close at hand.

## Chapter 18
## The Downfall of Uriah Heep

When I returned from Yarmouth, my aunt, Traddles, Mr Dick and I went down to Canterbury to keep our mysterious appointment with Mr Micawber.

"Mr Micawber, sir," said my aunt, "we are ready for Mount Vesuvius or anything else."

"I trust you will soon see an eruption," said Mr Micawber. "All I will say at this moment is that I have taken legal advice from Mr Traddles. I beg you to allow me a start of five minutes and then come to the

office of Wickfield and Heep and ask for Agnes."

Traddles merely smiled as Mr Micawber bowed and disappeared.

When five minutes had passed we went together to the old house without speaking. Mr Micawber feigned surprise at our arrival and led us into the dining room where he loudly announced our presence.

Our visit astonished Uriah Heep. He frowned so fiercely that he almost closed his eyes but he quickly smiled when Agnes came into the room.

"Don't wait, Micawber," said Heep, dismissing his clerk with a wave of his hand. Mr Micawber stood by the door.

"I told you to go," Heep yelled. "Why are you waiting?"

"Because I choose to do so," replied Mr Micawber. Heep turned pale.

"Oho! This is a conspiracy!" Heep cried, his face now red with rage.

"I am the agent and friend of Mr Wickfield," Traddles said quietly. "I have here his written authority to act for him in all matters."

"The old fool has drunk himself stupid," cried Heep. "You got it from him by fraud!"

"Something has been got by fraud, I know," said Traddles, "and so do you, Heep."

Heep's eyes glittered with hatred as he glared at us. Then Mr Micawber produced a letter from his pocket and read it aloud to us. It proved to be a detailed record of numerous malpractices committed by Heep since Mr Micawber had been his clerk. We learned that Heep had often forged Mr Wickfield's signature and falsified the accounts. Thus Heep had stolen Mr Wickfield's money and my aunt's investment too.

"And," said Mr Micawber triumphantly, "the forged documents are now in Mr Traddle's safe-keeping."

Heep made a dart at the letter, as if to tear it to pieces, but Mr Micawber struck his hand away.

"Uriah Heep," said Traddles, "you are to release Mr Wickfield from his partnership agreement with you immediately and you will also restore all the money you stole."

"I won't do it!" he shrieked.

"Perhaps you would prefer the law to punish you," said Traddles. "Copperfield, kindly fetch the police!"

"Stop!" Heep growled at me. "I'll do whatever you say."

"Good," said Traddles. "Now, Heep, you will stay in your room until we have examined all the papers and everything has been done to our satisfaction."

Mr Micawber was soon happily reunited

with his family and making plans for the future. At my aunt's suggestion, he decided to take his family to Australia with Mr Peggotty and Emily. With his future settled and his self-respect regained, Mr Micawber was again a happy man.

## Chapter 19
## Death and Darkness

Dora had grown weaker as the months passed. Did I know now, that my child-wife would soon leave me? The doctors had told me so but I clung to a lingering hope that she would be spared. One night, as I sat alone with her, she said with a gentle smile,

"I was not fit to be a wife, David. I was too young; not in years, but in experience and thoughts and everything. I was such a silly, little creature! Over the years you would have grown weary of me. It is better as it is."

"Oh, Dora, my dearest, do not speak to me so," I wept, "for we have been so very, very happy."

"Hush, my dear boy," she said softly. "Now, I want to speak to Agnes, alone."

While I sat by the fire with Jip at my feet, Agnes went to see Dora. The little dog whined to go upstairs.

"Not tonight, Jip! Not tonight!" I said.

The dog came slowly back to me and lay down at my feet. He stretched himself out as if to sleep and, with a mournful cry, was dead.

At that same moment, Agnes appeared, her face full of pity and grief, her cheeks wet with tears. It was over. My beloved Dora was dead.

So great was my grief that I came to think my life was at an end and that I could find refuge only in the grave. Then my aunt proposed that I should go abroad and seek

my peace in change and travel. I waited only for what Mr Micawber called 'the final pulverisation of Heep' and for the departure of the Peggottys and the Micawbers.

Aunt Betsey, Agnes and I returned to Canterbury and went to see Traddles at the Wickfield house. A heap of books and papers lay before him on the table.

"Miss Wickfield," said Traddles, "with Mr Dick's constant care your father has considerably improved and is more like his old self. I have checked through all the accounts and I find that there is sufficient money for your father to keep his business and his property. He is blameless of any wrong-doing."

"Oh, thank Heaven! His honour is restored," cried Agnes.

"Next, Miss Trotwood," said Traddles, "I am delighted to tell you that we have recovered all of your money from Uriah

Heep. He took it and kept it by him because he hated Copperfield and wanted to damage his prospects."

"He's a monster of meanness! What's become of him?" said my aunt.

"He has gone far away," said Traddles, "and we shall never see or hear from him again."

After Dora's death, my faithful old nurse, Peggotty, came to stay with me for a few days while her brother made his final travel preparations, for the time was drawing near for the sailing of the emigrant ship. Emily had written a farewell letter to Ham which I was to deliver to him.

"There's time for me to go and come back before the ship sails," I said. "I'll go this evening."

As I neared Yarmouth, a terrible storm was raging; the streets were strewn with sand and seaweed and crowds of people

were all running in one direction, to the beach.

"What is the matter?" I yelled above the noise of the wind.

"A wreck! Close by! A schooner from Spain. Make haste if you want to see her. She'll go to pieces any moment."

I ran down to the beach, and then I saw her, close in upon us! One mast was broken and lay over the side, entangled in a maze of sail and rigging. With great waves battering her sides the ship rolled violently and began to break apart. The sea swept over the rolling wreck and tossed men and casks and planks into the boiling surge.

The agony on shore increased for no one dare attempt a rescue in that tumultuous sea. Then I saw the people part and Ham come breaking through them towards the sea. I ran to stop him and held him back with both arms. But Ham was determined

to save the lone man who still clung to the mast – a man with dark, curly hair and a jaunty, red cap.

"Mas'r Davy," said Ham, firmly grasping me by both hands, "if my time has come, 'tis come. If it hasn't, I'll succeed. Lord above, bless you and bless all!"

I watched Ham dash into the sea with a rope tied around his waist. A great wave swept him back to land. He was hurt. I saw blood on his face but he paid no heed to that. Again, he fought his way towards the wreck and had almost reached it when a vast, green mountain of water hurled the ship to the bottom of the sea. The men pulled on the rope and drew Ham back to shore – to my very feet. Ham was dead; his generous heart was stilled for ever.

They carried him to the nearest house, and I remained with him. As I sat beside the bed, a fisherman who had known me when Emily and I were children, came and whispered my name.

"Sir," he said, his lips trembling, "will you come with me now?"

Then I remembered the sailor who had clung to the mast as the ship went down. I rose and followed the fisherman.

"Has a body come ashore?" I asked him, terror-stricken.

"Yes," he said, holding out an arm to support me.

"Do you know it?" I asked.

He said nothing but he led me to the shore. And on that part of the beach where, as children, Emily and I had looked for shells, I saw James Steerforth lying with his head upon his arm, as I had often seen him lie on his bed at school.

They laid Steerforth on a hand-bier and his old, sailing friends covered him with a flag and carried him from the beach. That night, I took his body home to Highgate and laid him in his mother's room. I lifted up his leaden hand and held it to my heart. And all the world seemed death and darkness.

## Chapter 20
## My Return to England and to Agnes

Peggotty and I went down to Gravesend to say our good-byes to the Peggottys and the Micawbers before they sailed for Australia. To our delight, we learned from Mr Peggotty that Martha was going too. She, Emily and Mr Peggotty would start a new life together.

Shortly after their departure I left England and spent the next three years travelling in Europe and writing. I sent my stories to Traddles who arranged for their publication very profitably for me. With the passage of

time my health had improved and I decided to return to England.

During my years abroad, Agnes had become very dear to me. Her letters to me had been soothing and cheerful, telling me that she was happy and gainfully employed, at the school she had opened for young girls. The more I thought about Agnes the more I knew how much I loved her and wanted to marry her.

I landed in London on a wintry, autumn evening and went immediately to see Traddles.

"How glad I am to see you!" he cried. "And grown so famous! My good Copperfield. And now, my friend, I'd like you to meet my wife. Sophy and I are married at last!"

I wished them happiness with all my heart. My aunt had long since returned to her cottage at Dover and Mr Dick and Peggotty lived with her. The next day, I went to see them and was greeted with tears of joy.

"Well, Trot," said my aunt when we were alone that evening, "when are you going over to Canterbury to see the Wickfields?"

"I shall go tomorrow, Aunt," I replied. "But tell me, is Agnes . . . is she married?"

"She might have married twenty times since you have been gone!" cried my aunt. "Indeed, Trot," she added with a knowing glance, "I think Agnes is going to be married."

I rode away very early the next day to see Agnes.

"Dear Agnes, how happy I am to see you once again!" I whispered tenderly and I held her to my heart. Presently, I spoke again,

"You have a secret, Agnes. Please share it with me for I care only for your happiness. I must hear from your lips what I have heard from others – that there is someone you will marry, someone to whom you have given

your love."

Agnes turned her pale face towards me and burst into tears.

"If I have any secret, I cannot share it," she sobbed. "It has been mine for years and must remain mine."

Suddenly, new thoughts and hopes whirled through my mind.

"Dearest Agnes!" I cried, clasping her in my arms. "I went away loving you and I returned home, loving you. I have always loved you, Agnes. Do I dare to hope . . .?"

"Oh, Trotwood, there is one thing I must say," said Agnes calmly. "My dear, I have loved you all my life."

We were married within a fortnight. Later, Agnes told me that on the night Dora died, her dying wish had been that only Agnes would take her place as my wife.

Agnes wept and I wept with her, though we were so very happy.

## Chapter 21
## A Visitor

As the years passed my fame as a writer grew and I became rich. Agnes and I had been married ten happy years. One evening in spring, when we were sitting by the fire in our house in London and three of our children were playing in the room, a servant announced the arrival of a stranger.

"Is he here on a matter of business?" I asked.

"No, he has come for the pleasure of seeing you," said the servant. "He is an old man and he looks like a farmer."

The children were eager to see the mysterious visitor.

"Let him come in here," I said.

There soon appeared in the doorway a sturdy, grey-haired, old man.

"Why, it is Mr Peggotty!" cried Agnes as she embraced him.

Once our first, happy greetings were over, Mr Peggotty sat before the fire with the children on his knees.

"The years pass and I don't grow younger," he said, "and it has always been on my mind that I must come and see Mas'r Davy afore I got to be too old."

"And now tell us," I said, "how you have all fared in Australia."

"Perhaps life was a little hard at first," he said, "but what with stock-farming and with sheep-farming we have prospered well since then."

"And Emily?" said Agnes and I together.

"The news of Ham's death had greatly saddened Emily. She was very depressed for a time but her farm work kept her busy. She could have married well a number of times since then but she chooses not to. 'Uncle,' she says to me, 'that's gone forever.' And now," he continued, "in addition to taking fond care of her uncle, my Emily spends her time teaching children and tending the sick and needy."

"Is Martha still with you?" I asked.

"No. She married a fine, young farmer some years ago," he replied.

"Now, last, though not least, Mr Micawber?" I said, smiling.

"He worked as a farmer for a few years," said Mr Peggotty, "but now he's a much loved and respected Magistrate in our town."

Mr Peggotty stayed with us for almost a month. Before he left, we went to Yarmouth to see the headstone on Ham's grave. While

I was copying the plain inscription for him, I saw him stoop and gather a tuft of grass from the grave.

"For Emily," he said as he put it in his pocket. "I promised, Mas'r Davy."

## Chapter 22
## Contentment

And now my written story ends. Here is my aunt, now more than eighty years old, but upright yet, and proud godmother to a real, living Betsey Trotwood, my daughter.

Always with her, here comes Peggotty, my old nurse. Her cheeks and arms are shrivelled now but my children grasp her rough forefinger as I once did. She carries something bulky in her arms; it is the crocodile book, dilapidated by this time, but my children read of the 'crorkindills' as I once did.